Remembering the Night Train

by

Shaida Mehrban

 **New Generation Publishing**

She searched for the night train,
way before I can remember.
Her life was like the rain,
in the cold black months after
September.
Her open books became the closed
pages,
as she sat in the night to read the
different stages.
The steam and the smoke were all
outside,
but her search became reality here
inside.
She tried really hard to keep this
madness at bay
and as she closed her eyes, the pain
forgot the day.
She tried really hard, so hard she tried
by washing the water that she had cried.
The mystery train had a warm exciting
vibe,
her emotions made sure that the wanting
was alive.
The bright sparks struck her engine
alight!
As her quest for wanting became her
really big fight.
Her love for him was like a dead slow
engine;
no steam or coal to keep it from

descending.
The feisty inside played the yearning
game
as the puffs of smoke ran slowly in vain.
The mother's eyes lit when the
engines sparked,
a father's life looked ready to be parked.
Her head filled with garbage that the
cold passengers left behind
and the sunken faces of empty dreams
yet to find!
Her hard body caressed the dark
cold night sky
and her tender hands touched the secrets
goodbye.
A life half empty or a life half full?
She scrubbed and scrubbed the
cracks of her dreams
he remembered her fraying away at the
seams.
She opened the shutter for the
calling of the winds
as I closed the window to mother's sins.
She smelt the things that I could not
see,
he sensed the noises that she wanted to
be.
I heard the whispers that she did not
breathe
as he sat sipping away at his stubborn

heave.
We heard the pins drop at the dining table,
but there was nothing in our palm that made us able.
We heard her dead voice against our deaf ears
as she painted her smile against our darkest fears.
Her tongue swirled smoothly into her coffee cup
his legs started to shiver as he held onto his tea mug.
He liked the silence as it felt like home
as she left him with an empty page and so much unknown.
She was the loser that won life's little races,
as the night train stopped to pick up her pieces.
Her eyes glowed brightly in the darkness of the night,
whilst boarding the night train it all seemed quite right.
Her heart thumped as the engines rattled and stirred,
as her soul paced to the voices unheard.
Her lips quivered to the unfound life
as the strangers in here are all still rife.

Her breath sighed at the site of the
tunnel
the light was lit when the night train did
rumble.
The hair on his nape did stand and
stare
at the rejection and empty life where no
one really did care.
She stood tall and strong for the
world to see,
deep down inside he was a broken man
to me.
He wore the masks that she did make
as he sits so quietly as if life is all fake.
She searches for the night trains
journey to end
as he asks, will life give him a helping
hand.

Chapter 1

The first time I saw him, it was amongst a blur in between the heavy fog surrounding the thick, smoggy London sky, in the middle of winter. A grey blanket overshadowed the tall grey concreted college building but as my gaze lowered against the backdrop of the sky and the building, there he stood still amongst his friends. They were mostly chattering away, but he stood silent as he looked on. His slim, almost delicate fingers making waves through his hair, he tossed his head to the left and then he met my gaze. He held that thought for ages, totally unaware almost of his friends, he looked besotted and I was smitten. I was totally unaware of the winter's cold now, as my heart started beating a little faster, like a child trying to run before it can walk, and my smile became much wider. Suddenly, a cold breeze overpowered my senses, leave a warm tear to fall from my eyes onto my cheek. It reminded me of the horrid past and the fact that the one thing that I didn't want was to be like my mother. I could not hurt my father like she did and I definitely didn't know that he was going to overpower my senses beyond belief.

That day was the first time our eyes met and from then to now, six months later, we had spoken to one another many times, but today was the first time that we were going to go out together. I was foolish and naïve and so very young, but then I was only eighteen. I know, that innocent girl living within me had a desired yearning to be found, since that day, not that long ago. Matty, my mother, short for Mathilda Martins, hated this name and always insisted on her being called Matty, had also been influenced by others in a search for the child who had grown up far too quickly into a woman to be found. She often said that my father had told her to mature out. Since then marriage and her lust and longing for the new, unfound her, had cost her marriage and our life which I yearned for as a child. My journey had yet to begin as my search continued and for what exactly? I didn't know, her search for that train with an unknown destination that will always travel at night. This day would change me and how I view the world? If my father had told me this, I would never have believed him, just like her, she didn't believe him either, but she always spoke of the train in the dark, that she will catch one day.

As I sat thinking about what I was going to wear, what Matty used to wear, I sat in vain, in anticipation, shaking my legs all the while, an almost naughty-but-nice experience. I stared at the wardrobe as I gently wiped away the spot of dust on the right shelf. Slowly, I lowered my gaze onto the small hanging, soldier-like rails. I fumbled through the brightly-coloured jackets, the yellow, the grey, the reds and the blacks, they all resembled a timely mood. Yes, today, I will wear the red busty, the sun's shining, it's hot outside, so why not inside and within? I can choose what to wear but it is not easy to tell father where and why I am going out on a weeknight. Father Jack, that's what she insisted that I call him so, as a child, I grew up calling my own dad Father

Jack, but his real name was Jacob Murray. Jacob's Creek, Jacob biscuits, mysterious until touched, explored, tasted or even sweet like Murray Mints but my father was the latter of these, he was uncomplicated, what you saw was what you got. He didn't say what he didn't mean, he weighed up his words before they could burden someone and he didn't beat around the bush either, so unlike my mother.

The wooden gate outside was creaked, almost like the shriek of the train stopping, and I quickly gathered my thoughts and went to the window. I pulled the curtain briskly aside. There he was burdened with a heavy shopping bag again, his left shoulder sliding lower than the right as the big strong bag haggled near the ground. He shows no strain on his face. The merry men follow him inside the house. I open my bedroom door to listen to the soft scratching of big feet on the withered coarse straw mat. His loud echoing but strong voice in the distance as he opens the front door, the others with their gentle dust gathering voices almost whispery and withered as they all make their way slowly into the living room. My father and his friends have all come inside.

The noise of a soft pitter-patter step and then the clumpiness of his big feet dragging against the hob-nailed hardwood of the stairs and then he calls "Lilly Roe, what are you doing love?" I stayed silent, he doesn't persist, but then I know that I should go and tell him first, get it over and done with really. I know the outcome, he will web his words together emotionally so that I will feel bad, firstly because I am going against his wishes on a weeknight and secondly because he would like me to help him, which I cannot today. I know, I will get ready first and then face the gentle giant. The guilt is already scratching beneath my soul. I can see his lips curl upwards as his gaze follows the lines along the wooden grain of the floor, straight, but there is no hardness in him. What is he thinking now? If only I could reach where she could not. I cannot hear the thumping of his pain but I can feel it within my body. I have never felt his wet tears ever, but they have always made my throat heavy, he has always reached out to me, but without ever putting his hand out. I have to stop the reminiscing and get ready to go out.

An hour later and I am fully ready now. I make my way down the stairs, my feet, one after the other, slowly step off the creaky step on the middle of the stairs, I reach the bottom. I stop just outside the living room and I listen. I close my eyes but I can almost see the flame-lit mustang stick, the smell of the burning bark, yes, my father was smoking his cigar as always. I put my nose almost to the crack of the door, he quickly opens it, "Come on in, Lilly Roe dear." Just behind him, I can sense the smoke of the cigar sweeping past my shoulder and a strong musky peppermint chewing gum smell follows his kind smile. The room is full of warming mellow smells, so homely and comforting.

My father steps aside, the delicate chattering of the small crowd, their eyes blue, grey and black, mysteriously searching the newspaper headlines, always ready to read something bad. I stare at them, the gentlemen's perfectly criss-crossed legs fold the lining on the clouded and somewhat shiny ashy-grey trousers, they remain silent and still. I catch a glance of my father's smoky far away drifting eyes as I gently tell him that I cannot stay and help him and I am going out. He stops his gaze and without a flicker, he moves his body slowly onto the big armchair in the corner, out of the way, where she always sat. "Alright, Lilly Roe" was all he said. I quietly closed the living room door behind me, and stood cold and alone. His peppermint breath lingered all the way down to my backbone, almost as if he was still keeping me standing straight and strong an even though I cannot see him anymore, I can feel his sadness clearly within my bones.

I tried to forget about my father for a while because I had to focus on my first real date and I couldn't let any disappointment get in the way. I was eighteen and he was twenty-four and even though we were both studying at the same college, our paths were in the opposite direction. I was the girl who went to college to better my future life, and he was the rich kid who went to college to pass time. Suddenly the muzzled ring of the doorbell clanging, chased the noise like the white doves all rushing into the cold air. My spine felt a small tremor as I reached for the front door.

I slowly feel the cold smoky damp brassy door handle of this heavy-burden door and like the heavy train that burdens the weight of all unknown passengers, I slowly stroke smooth my shirt. My shirt should look perfect, just like him. My feet straddle along the warm-smelling sweet carpet, not dirty, just used and the more I pull my stride, the more the smell of home, rich, wooden, smoky, stale but lingering roasted kernel, nutty aroma beneath my feet, a constant reminder of the cigarette fumes we breathe every day. It's strong and masculine, like my father, so why did my mother hate it so much? Had her train ticket come?

I take a deep breath as I quickly grab the brass knob, the coldness of the metal brings me back to life. I am fully awake now, as I slowly pull the knob and there he was standing like a breath of fresh air. I don't know whether it's the cold from the outside breeze even though it's summertime or whether there's a chill within me. I still don't know but it has definitely awoken a delicate fear or a search for the unknown within me. It's almost as if all that excitement, all the wanting, the eagerness, it's not all the wanting, the eagerness, it's not that clear anymore and yet, he is standing in front of me, my eyes see him clearly, even though my eyes do not meet his, but what do they meet? My nose has smelt his delicate almost sweet almond-smelling body and yet I have not touched him but it's strange how before all that, I sensed, almost felt his touch on my hand and yet we had never even held hands.

"Ain't you ready yet, baby girl?" As

I hear the word "baby" I feel a pulling sensation within my own belly button, the umbilical cord was fighting to free the child from the mother so I thought, but I had wished that the fighting struggle was to keep hold of me for longer within these walls. I go straight to the laundry room, lift off my mac from the metal grey hook that is tainted with the old smell of the mould, damp cord, not lived in, old and uncared for, wishing that the mac had not come off the hook. It has, so I then put it on even though I am wearing my red busty and it doesn't look as if it's going to rain, but I am still feeling cold. I look at the top button of my coat, its red button withering from the constant use, the button hole, abused, overworked, pulled like the thread from the bobbin into the needle. The red thread seems lifeless today like its owner, afraid but also racing nervous.

"Hey, my baby girl, move it," he

said with a slow yet commanding tone that drills deep down into the pores of my skin. My face dampens. I look around and as I face him, his stare deepens and just like Jekyll and Hyde, suddenly he mellows and I begin to see his gold tooth shining. He does have a tempting, inviting smile, warm, like the logs on the fire, the heat tempting enough for me to get close. "Hurry, hurry" was all I remember. He held my hand neatly and snuggly into his but like a balaclava on top of the face that is finding it hard to breathe, I slam the front door behind me and we both walk side-by-side, his powerful feet in control, striding wide and precise unlike my own and could it be that I just wasn't sure of all this and he played me like the violin that was dying to be played?

We roam the slow walk along the busy London sheets, the upright lengthy buildings, old and gracious and yet still beautiful, the roads full of wavy hairstyles flowing like the sand on the dunes, pretty bright colours parading along the footpaths and lots and lots of curvaceous, slender, masculine and some even covered legs walked, all of them in a hurry. Why is it they all followed each other as if all these people had a final destination in sight? My destination was a destiny that someone else had arranged, a mission that had been filled with an array of distinguished colours and tainted smells like poppies and roses of reds and yellows, and the sun's heat and the green storks resemble the evergreen land. I was just one example of these beauties and that is what he always said to me.

"Where are we going to?" I kept asking and he kept saying the same thing, "Just wait and see." Soon there was a plague of people like swarms of bees and wasps buzzing away making a nuisance of themselves, smashing themselves on the windows of the shops, hurling shoes, sticks, bricks and that tiny small piece of liquorice caressing the little boys' rubber sole as he sits restlessly on the floor, then he smudges its remains and slowly slithers it along to get rid of it, but he knows he is facing a losing battle. There is so much worse, shouting like the fans of Manchester United winning against the Gunners in an away match, but this doesn't feel like a win. A woman helplessly pushes her pram as fast as her legs allow but amidst the big crowds she finds it impossible to reach safety. I ask my boyfriend why people are destroying and looting the shops, why are they stealing goods, smashing the windows, kicking furniture around and with no fear but instead with excitement. The fear I see so clearly, the helpless, out of control young men attacking and being attacked by the big bodies of the authority, their batons ready to strike, their shields offering them very little shelter possible. My boyfriend pulls me into the crowd.

I look down, my razzle dazzle, lots of glitter, bit of a wedge with killer heels, so specially warm and generic-like fur, shiny like the brightness of the moon, shining like the galaxy in the sky and the heels to give me height to reach up to Tony. I pick the speed up in my feel and trot along, against my knowledge and wishes, I didn't even know about it, but what is all this? I hasten my pace but he has his grip tight on me like the dog lead that gets tied onto the collar of the bitch even though, with speed, she may get loose from the owner but never from the tag. He looks at me and I keep repeating "What is all this?" He keeps saying "Shut up, shut up."

Chapter 2

My legs graze against a brick wall of a shop, my new tights rip like the ladder that has a few climbed steps and I'm wishing that I had not worn my mac because it's definitely still dry today. Just my red jacket would have been sufficient. My free arm reaches my brow to wipe the dripping sweat. I look at the remains of the colour base which apparently is called "foundation" on the sleeve tainted with black streaks and a dab of red. Foundation, isn't that the strong base that houses and buildings are built on, the mascara I suppose is the lashings of paint, thick like the alpine forest, lush and long, the red thick smudge of plastered lipstick topped with an overcoat of gloss.

I look at his ear, moving ever so slightly like the sudden twitch of a feather, but then he often does this when he's angry. The excitement has made his forehead wet as the sweat drips like the slow drip of the tap. He slowly brings his lashes down and blinks away, as he shakes his head to sway the wet fringe off his forehead, he looked so divine. His arms sway back and forth as his strides get faster and faster and so does the moisture under his armpits. His perfectly pressed shirt is crisp and yet under the swaying arms, it shows the fragments of the shirt which has been worn a few times.

He lets go of my hand suddenly, as I

look on to see that he had been hit by a stone, thrown by someone in the massive crowd. He keeps looking around to detect who had thrown it at him, but it was impossible to know. He starts swearing, "You f***ing this and you f***ing that, what b*****d has hit me?" What was the point of it, within the crowd, everyone has to look after themselves but more so to cause havoc for others. I can see his left cheek brightening up which resembled the anger he was feeling. His nostrils a little flared showing shades of a few almost baby hairs, so delicate. He bends over and picks up some stones from the road. The cars have deserted the road, they obviously have been directed to a safer route. He throws the stones but they miss their goal and then I just stand and watch alone. I move across to the other side of the street and look on, I feel safer and yet my head can hear the train that will come in the night.

Tony is angrily pushing another young man. They don't know each other and yet they are busy pointing their figures and hands at one another, whilst pushing and shoving, but then this culture that is created here is exactly that, he is not doing anything that is different. Youngsters like us versus the oldies. What chance did the oldies have against us, they didn't expect to be attacked and yet the young adults seemed to have planned this, the guilty against the innocent, what was the purpose of this? I look at Tony, he's now moved on but I can still see him at a distance, he is standing just outside a shop, two people are standing inside the shop and I guess that they work there, workers who had not anticipated this day. They have come to serve their customers again today, to complete their wish of how every customer is always right, in a hope that every person who enters the store has their ambition fulfilled and so leave happily. The workers have done another great day of making more money for their employer, who In return may not recognise their hard work but, leaves it as an expectation for workers' performance to be better all the time, whilst he goes to feed his own family with the wealth he has made today.

Scared and bewildered, that's how they looked, the young mob have kicked the store's glass front with their feet, others are pushing, hurling abuse and hitting, thumping and shouting at whatever comes in their way. Someone in a dark-coloured top, almost purple, has thrown a packet of some white dust. A can of white something has flown into the air and landed back down, scattered and splattering everywhere, his own purple top is discoloured anew but he is still bopping up and down as he steadily moves along. But the crowd have not stood still either, a few are fleeing the scene, some are throwing themselves into the crowd, some dispersing like the mosquitos into thin air, the shrills of the terror in the innocent victims' voices, the aching heart as if it's being pulled out, seen in the face of the middle-class lady in her orange stripy almost Jasper Conran shoulder handbag dumped beside her, her head scarf covering her dignity as she leans on the pavement, helpless, her elbow digging into the concrete path, she looks down.

I look at them all, the chattering of voices, the noise of people moving from north to south. I feel the fright within the core of my belly. It's a feeling that I cannot associate myself with but, it is as I am living it. Then suddenly, I am consoled by the men and women who have power and authority, somehow the tall policemen seem to have the edge of power, the female policewoman seems to be doing exactly what the others are, but they are not scared of her and she doesn't make me feel that calm will be created anytime soon. The mob ignore her as she tries to restores order by shouting in a loud, authoritative, peace-keeping voice which no one listens to, her arms out to protect herself. The handcuffs strapped to her clothes waiting to strike their next law-breaking victim.

She pushes her black and white hat even more firmly on her head and moves in and out between people, trying so hard to restore peace. I know that there is fighting going on and that people are attacking each other verbally or physically, but more to the fact that there are too many people in a small place and as time goes by, the frustration and the tiredness of the day is making some almost violent, others scared and a few helpless. Where are they all heading and what is all this rioting and looting about and more to the point, what is Tony doing here and why? I stand and wonder into the far away horizon where the sky and the pavement's heat sizzle, so far away where the blue merges with the white blurry clouds of dust and then become one, inseparable! That's me and Tony!

I try to see where he is but now there is no vision of him at all, the crowded street has had no cars on it, just a jungle of people running senselessly about making a nuisance of themselves. That policewoman, I can see her, she is also with her own crowd now, the police are out in full force, mostly chasing the youngsters. The victims who have been attacked are like the prey that are scared of being attacked again helplessly and the perpetrators, who should be scared, are acting like heroes, as if they are putting the world to rights and as for the police, well, they are the peace-keepers and they are finding today difficult and are undermined. The ambulance and fire brigade are on the scene but they cannot get to the injured or the burning.

Within this riot, the police remain helpless, their eyes peering to see sight of this not ending as they search for the light at the end of the tunnel, their eyes like the stars in the galaxy, the helpless girl trying to escape the ever-increasing danger almost as if she is afraid of her own fragile existence, afraid of being a woman. The young kid, so very young, fearless, roaring like the fierce lioness, her arms up in the air as she passes me, hurling like the venom from a snake's mouth, the tongue slithery and slimy, her top, short and showing her tiny waist carefully dimpled with the flat pierced belly button. She takes no notice of the opposition who are now using force nor of the shopkeeper who is pleading to be left alone and not taunted by harassment or even by the lady who was trying to protect herself, her twisted shoe, the scuffed heel, my gaze shortens its distance and I look at my own shoes.

I try to make sense of it once again but why is it that I don't understand what this is all about, I am an innocent outsider, but who am I, what am I doing here? I stand still but now I can feel that it's going to get ugly now, the police will come to me with questions and accusations wanting me to paint a colourful intricate picture for them, but I am not an artist. They'll want me to be placed in the eyes of the lady justice so that I can agree with what they say and the man with the big curly powerful wig will want to make sense of it all. I cannot make sense of it all, how will anyone else? My blue watery eyes have witnessed it but my head cannot put the rubic cube into order, the yellows, greens, blues and reds are scattered everywhere and yet each one of these has a purpose of belonging with the others. My heart flutters delicately like the small waves of white fluff in the sky, it's panicking as if my ears have heard the bells toll at the top of the hour, but my heart has felt it. It's the aching tingling heart within me that sees the dark, smoky black man in his rumpled shirt and striking big white smile and then he is overtaken by fear of the unknown and his mouth slowly closes with fear, a closed button only to be replaced by the thick lines on his forehead running straight across like the sturdy train track, strong and long, lines of stress, a sturdy train track line carrying the night train along.

I take my mac off and sling it on my arm. I turn around and I start walking back home. I cannot recollect the exact route that I had trod but it didn't take that long, so I am sure that I will get home even after getting lost a few times. I looked at the road signs to see if my town or street name was on there, but it wasn't. I asked a lady and she was not sure. I asked a big strong man and he gently replied that he doesn't live around here. I wasn't afraid or sad but maybe happy because the further I got from the noise, the better I felt. The more I walked, the clearer the roads seemed, the more familiar my surroundings got, the slower my heart paced.

As I narrowed closer to my road, I could feel the sense of sigh and relief all the way to my fingertips, it was a tremendous feeling. I quietly slide my fingers around the slithery door knocker and give it a thick dull bang almost like a horse's gallop. My father's silvery hair, combed high and to the side, can be seen through the frosted glass pane of the door as he gently walks to the front door where I stand. I hear him softly clearing his throat as he pulls the door ajar. He is looking straight at me, into my eyes but with so many question marks on his forehead. Finally, he blurts out the obvious question, after all I had rehearsed the answers to his questions all the way home and now that I am finally home, the words just cannot find their way out. Instead, I shake my head slowly, and he understands that I don't want to talk about it and he asks no more as he lowers his light-brown lashes and nods to say he understands.

Quietly, lifeless and with a mind full of questions and no answers now, I climb the stairs. Somehow the stairs seem to be much longer today as if there are more steps for my tired legs to climb, but I consoled my mind that I have climbed these steps so often that they are exactly the way they always have been except for one thing, I cannot smell the tainted smell of tobacco anymore. That seemed really strange because it was the first time that they smelt of nothing and I smelt of the outdoors. My fist clenched tightly as it hit the closed bedroom door. I move into my bedroom and suddenly everything has closed me off from the outside world. I kick off my shoes and notice the tiniest toenail polish ruined, the other toes still look perfect like this morning except for the fact that they look sore and wrinkly. I throw my mac and free my arm to take the red jacket off, the red showed its colour today and yet this was not the real me. I look into the mirror, but I don't recognise the person in front of me!

I stare and stare with tears rolling down my cheeks in search of something but I don't know what. I rub my hand over my tearful eyes to erase the day's events but all I see is the runny mascara and its streaks. I wipe it away with the sleeve of my top, but it only marks the clothing as well. My crying silences but the tears roll on steadily as I lay on my bed looking up at the ceiling. The small lines of the sturdy ceiling smooth over into the corner where the white flakes of paint have become crisp and tight. I look at my shoes, they look as if they have seen better days. They look crisp, harsh and tight. I rub my feet which felt good, so comforting. It feels good as if the pain has all gone from the tired feet. My hands need washing now but that will have to wait, as I close my eyes.

Chapter 3

The aches and pains in my feet feel so much better in the morning as I wake to the streaming sun, radiating my room and giving it heat, colour and warmth. I look at the clock in my room as the big hand strikes at the top of the hour and the small hand stays steady as if it's not moved in a very long time from the eight. I get up, go to the bathroom and have a quick shower. I rinse the shower tray and I know that father has already rinsed his body as I can see silver-grey hair in the sieve in the corner of the tray. I don't like him cleaning my mess, because that's the woman's chore, cooking but especially cleaning. I quickly get dressed as I can smell the aroma of the splattering eggs and tomatoes sizzling in the sizzling fat pan. My father doesn't ever like to eat by himself. If no one accompanies him, he doesn't eat, that's why he calls his friends over quite a lot. If he knows that I am in for dinner, he doesn't often call them and as for lunch times, he will always have a quick sandwich in front of the television watching the daytime programmes, watching his life go by.

"Come in Lilly Roe, breakfast is ready. Hope you're hungry girl?" he says quickly with his back to the kitchen door.

"How did you know I was in the room, father?"

"Lilly Roe, I don't need eyes to see you to know that you are in my presence girl. I can sense you, my heart feels your warmth even before you have entered the room, the gentle pitter-patter of your soft tiny feet. I can feel the soft butterfly gently moving around the enormous space and you know girl the most unpredictable thing of all, the way you always slide your right hand slowly behind the nape of your neck and then as you slide your hand away, you always touch your earlobe and then your hand is down beside your hips, am I right, Lilly Roe?"

"Father, why, I have never noticed myself doing this ever, but I know one thing for sure father and that is no matter what happens, you are always here." I watch father as he quietly pushes the small chair out of my way so that I can get in between the dining table comfortably. I quietly stand at the

45

table and bend slowly whilst pulling the chair close to my legs. He pushes the back of my chair with his big foot, crushing his big toe until the chair sat neatly into the slotted position where it stays all day, like a tea cup slotted perfectly in the middle of the saucer.

"Well Lilly Roe, all in good time, all in good time girl."

"I'm not a good time girl, father."

He quickly looks at me as if he was reading what I had never intended saying. His brows narrowed, his gaze deepens and then he slowly looks down, the brows wider and the dipped arch, three quarters of the way of the brow, quickly pushes up to open up the eyes and yet he's looking down, his lashes thin and long enough for the colour of his eye and the clear white to shine through. Now I know I have to tell him because that disappointed look in his eyes has mellowed me and it's always like that. I just cannot keep a secret and certainly not from him! My teeth grind together like wheels in motion as I quickly utter out "Well father...." He quickly looks up at me and moves his hand across onto my shoulder, he places it hard and with authority but then calmly butts in with a smile and "Let's eat girl, we will talk it over later, just enjoy." I smiled at him and his smile follows mine, as he quietly sits next to me. We sit in silence comfortably and tuck into our breakfast almost as if we had not eaten in a while.

We hear the crunchy white bakery toast so perfectly brown, melted Anchor butter mellowed between our tongues and teeth. Silence is so golden, the crunch, the churning of food in my father's wide mouth and the gentle breakfast programme easing us into the new day, guests coming and going on the breakfast sofa. Now the news has come on and suddenly the calm on the television has come to an end but at our breakfast table the forks have been laid down on the plate, the crunching has stopped and the spoon in the tea cup has stopped turning. I didn't really understand what they were saying but something about a peaceful protest in Tottenham after the death of Mark Duggan, described as a local man shot by the police on 4th August 2011. The riot that took place last night, a 16 year old young man pushed and punched by officers, on the scene, police, buses, homes and businesses all getting coverage, the devastation caused by the looting and most of all, young people causing a nuisance, disruption and devastation to innocent people and businesses.

My father sighs with a slow tut-tut. I look at him and then he says, "Don't these young hooligans have anything better to do than to cause devastation and what are all the demonstrations for? Why don't they sit at the table and talk things through in a civilized manner, after all they are the adults of tomorrow." He looks at me, his eyebrows, whisky and raised and then he snaps sharply, "I blame the parents, they haven't taught their children well. They don't all sit at the table to eat together, so when do they teach their children family morals? I just hope you, Lilly Roe, never do anything like that ever. Always, always stay away from trouble, walk away, just walk away."

"Calm down father. I did walk away, promise I didn't do anything. I didn't get involved, I walked away as you have taught me father." Suddenly there was no reply, no response, just a stillness, an eerie kind of discomfort. My eyes follow his stillness but I don't look up. He stands but looks away from me, he looks away from the television and drifts his stare at the open window. What is he thinking, is he going to shut it, the window, why the window, he's drifting in his thoughts, his hands in his pockets. So still, he moves a few steps, takes his hands out and places them on his waist, his thumbs clicking against his shirt whilst the fingers firmly lay still. I know he is angry as his legs always shake a little when he is stressed and his trousers always move a tiny bit. A few minutes later, the shaking stops, he clears his throat with a small slow cough, then crosses his arms and slowly stirs his body towards me. He looks straight at me and it's almost as if I can see the blue horizon full of words, but all he says is "Good Lilly Roe, good." He unfolds his arms and raises his long big finger and directs it at me whilst sternly moving it up and down.

After breakfast, father's mind was

elsewhere as he just didn't seem himself, he didn't whistle whilst washing up or listen to the radio, Radio 2 as normal, it should have been delightfully quiet and yet in my ears I had heard the deafening roar of the night before. It haunted me most of the night when I was woken up many times with my spine chilled by the roar of the fiery words, the loud cold screams of the menacing acts and the fear in the eyes of many. This crowd violently controlled the streets without a care in the world. The disruption was bad and destructive, with hooligans controlling or being controlled themselves by their own actions and yet no one heard the train merrily speeding away without losing its momentum, but I heard then and during the night.

All day long I tried hard to avoid my father and in our small house, it wasn't as easy. Father stayed in the kitchen diner where we don't just cook and eat, but it's also the place where we sit, an absolute gem of a room, an all in one, which even included a television. The sitting room which only acted as a host to visitors was always very inviting but strangely enough none of us used it. The comfortable sofas of beige and gold perfectly lined around the room with the middle showing a fluffy white rug tussled on the brown carpet cradling underneath the heavy marble table and the ashtray perfectly placed in the centre of the table. Apart from these two rooms, there were only two bedrooms left, my father and mother's and that was the master bedroom and mine, a small almost box room. A box which I slept in the four walls turquoise, green and blue, rippling with my life, then waves going up and down like the emotions in my own.

Even though I had wanted to go and

hibernate in my bedroom, I didn't do so because father always gets more moody and even though I feel sorry for myself and think that he is moody and angry at me, I know deep down inside he is feeling lonesome, no one to share that time with, a problem halved is a problem that's been shared and he doesn't hold a grudge. Once he has aired his linen he will happily wear them so once he has made peace by speaking his mind, he will move on. He misses her existence without mentioning her, he caresses the chair which she always sat on as he leaves his own and keeps the chipped mugs of hers rather than throwing them away and yet, he's too proud to talk about it. Talking, words going round and round, those spoken with passion and love have got him nowhere, those that involved his hand striking the table were gestures of frustration but which fell on deaf ears, his words of wisdom for those who didn't want free advice, what are words and who is even bothered in listening to any of it?

The day dragged like the white line on the straight wide road that never ends, whilst in between we both rearranged to nibble a ploughman's lunch, without uttering any words to one another. The clock, busy as ever, eternal chime on the top of the hour, it struck and my gaze lifted. It was six o'clock. The heavy short plump hand lazily dragging itself to the next hurdle, the minute hand, strong and sturdy making it to the end of every hour with relief and then there's the second hand that never seems to falter, its nimble light quickly circles the orbit of the clock. I look away but from the corner of my eye, I could still see the second hand resisting all temptation. The striking has started again, how could that be? My father suddenly opens the door and half enters the doorway of the kitchen, abruptly he speaks, "Your friend has come, again, he is waiting in the hall." He leaves but the door's ajar. I quicken my pace and then hasten, I stand behind the open door not knowing what I am going to say, what do I want to say to him, what would be the point of saying anything? Quietly and slowly, I walked towards him.

I look at him, straight into his eyes, mine showed pain and betrayal, his showed no pain, remorse or regret. I stood a few feet away from him, hoping for an apology, but it was not forthcoming. He looked, his eyes deep but very still, his mouth watery and moist, his nostrils awakened by the sight of me in his presence. I was standing still. Breathtakingly gorgeous, that was him. I was staring at him, still smitten by him even though I had seen another side of him that I hadn't liked, but maybe, just maybe, he was the person I was originally smitten by. His eyes started to smile as his lips became wider, the shiny glint in his eye warmed me, I was his once again. He cleared his throat and put his hand out to me. The silky smooth light brown, almost gingery hair popping out from his sleeve, smothered his skin, his light olive skin, fair and smooth, his fingers big and bony and the hand controlling as if he could capture and contract me. "Hey baby girl, come on, get ready, let's go out, have fun," he said warmly.

"Okay" was all I could possibly say. I looked at him, his hair plastered against his forehead, slick and straight and gorgeous, I did as I was told. My gaze lowered as I turned away to go and get ready, my eyes met his squeaky clean shoes, shiny and pointy as if worn for the very first time, the same as my black eye-liner, shiny, black and pointy at the end and perfectly precise as if freshly worn. I think I acquired this precision after seeing my own mother, she always had that fresh-look face, even without any make-up on. She just had that gifted, glowing, fresh complexion. Father always told her to go and get ready even if it was to go to the local shops, as she always did. Clean shaven every day, smart trousers and perfect pressed shirt and how could a gentleman go out without his hat! The gentleman who always opened the doors for women and the young, who always moved behind me now, was not a gentleman at all, looked like it but didn't behave like it. So why couldn't that one word come out of my mouth? No! Why couldn't he make it better by saying "Sorry"?

Quickly I got my mac and quietly faced him once more and once again he extended his hand out to me. Although I was saying "No, no" in my mind, my hand found its way straight into his like the baby in the cradle, slowly comforted, that's how I must have looked, so desperate. He pulled the door ajar now and as the soft mellow breeze swept through my fingers, the aromatic smell of the mustard, strong and pungent, swirls of smoky smell swept through my senses, I take my other hand and capture the smell and place it closer to my nose. I close my eyes and see the swirls creating a halo around me, it keeps me safe, it's my father's cigar.

Chapter 4

I slide my long finger onto his palm
and it twines with his delicate
whispery hair. He clasps my hand
tightly and leads and like a dog I
follow my keeper. My mouth feels the
chill of the air, but it's not cold, as I
burst out quickly, "I'm going out for a
while father. I won't be late though
father, is that okay?" I hear the
smudged reply almost like an echo, "If
you insist, Lilly Roe, if you insist, but
remember, remember."

With that, I look away from the house, towards the big horizon. I clear my throat and ask where we are going. He gently replies "Oxford Street". This make me smile because it's almost as if this big cloud has been lifted and today will be good, the famous shopping street for the rich, the not-so-rich and then there's us, the lower end of the scale, the Primark shoppers, the Superdrugs make-up counter customers and the ones who often will pick up the sandwich off the shelf to bridge the gap until dinner time and for indulgence sake, a take-away tea or coffee with a sticky bun, but that's fine, Oxford Street is great. We walk and walk and it's almost an hour now. It seems to have taken forever but finally we get there.

The screaming cars have all gone home, the customers have fled and some still fleeing the area, shopkeepers' eyes show fear and anticipation. They are open wide, noses pressed to the window, lips chattering in fear and abuse, an old man sits waiting for the world to go by in the corner café which is still open or is it his own and he is fearless rather than fearful? His coffee cup shivers as he looks from the top of the cup and slowly slurps a long sigh and then slowly puts the cup down perfectly into its saucer. He pays special attention to all the ladies who walk by, not men, boys or girls, but mature over-forties women as his eyes follow them from the feet all the way up to the top of the head. He is callous and doesn't care if anyone sees him. We walk past him and he doesn't look at us even though I do.

We have been waiting for over an hour now and there seems to be a slow build-up of the same commotion that I witnessed last night, it's almost as if last night's news was on repeat today, but then how can that be because that was yesterday? I was there and my father wasn't happy and today, it's becoming the same again and I am once again here, but I smile for I know that he won't let go of my hand, he wouldn't, not again. A policewoman has slowly crept up from behind us somewhere and looks straight at us. Tony quickly pushes me against the wall, he pulls me toward him from my waist as his arm cradles me perfectly into his tight grip. He puts his nose to mine and then he moves his lips to smooth over mine but I slowly tilt my cheek to him and his lips smother my left cheek. I look over his nose from the top of his forehead but his eyes are enjoying the caress, the policewoman looks no further at us and moves on. I happily enjoy this like a devil as my smile widens from the right side and even though his lips press my cheek tightly I can still feel his facial hair tickling my cheek, soft and subtle, sweet and sensuous.

The policewoman has gone but still he is controlling my body and my senses, the body with his arm and senses with his lips and I was totally unaware that I was also doing the same. I let him caress my cheek and whilst convincing myself that I was "not bothered or enjoying it" this was so far from the truth and as for his body, well I had my hand firmly on his back, it had found the warmth comforting and so tight and close to me, the way it used to be with mother but never with father. Father always cuddled the way a father dies, so typical, big hug with a big smile but I could always sense his feet to be quite far from mine, everything was not touching, like a perfect decent gentleman. As for my mother, she hugged and squeezed as if it gave her mind and soul comfort but it gave father happiness within his own heart.

Happiness or a need but Tony was almost hugging for sexual pleasure, but this pleasure I had never seen nor sensed.

My senses awoke and slowly I put my hand between me and him, next to his heart, he understood and slowly he looked down and then away, his lingering look with his eyes continued to stare at me in an unbelievable sensual manner and he finally said "Sorry" and slowly started clearing his throat and moving to the side once again. He took my hand and edged me on to start walking or standing beside her man in spite of everything, like "troublesome Bonny and menacing Clyde", but not like "romantic Romeo and idolising Juliet", almost like "cops and robber" but not like crumpled Columbo and the talk of his absent bellowed wife.

I then asked what we were doing here and he quietly replied that we were going to meet his mates. I didn't say a thing but my head nodded ever so slightly, but then he wasn't really interested in my response at all. We got to the tube station when suddenly he started to wave, there were glimpses of young people coming towards us, lots and lots of young men and women, well-groomed and well-dressed, bringing a lot of noise with them. All of a sudden the noise where we were standing seemed minimal because it was overtaken by the big group coming towards us. A young boy at the front with a brown side bag, saddling it in position on his left hip, holding hands with the young girl with the wavy mousy hair, swinging his arms in victory even though they were burdened with a rucksack on her back and her red nose stud showing the devil in her temperament, I didn't like what I saw!

The scene was almost like what I

had seen on the television early this morning and once again, I was at a similar scene and today will be yesterday's news yet again. The same squeaking of the shrilling voices of terror, the street deserted by cars and full of people. Innocent bystanders looking across the street, a woman stands in horror absorbing the street that has started off by innocent shoppers who were out with their indulgent moods plastered on their faces and then they have disappeared and this street now has been invaded by young people looting, shouting, screaming and making a nuisance of themselves and for those around them. They bear no grudge or resistance against others because they don't think of the outcome of what they are doing.

I have been standing here for at least an hour and have watched the self-destruction of this street. Young men and women, girls and boys on the rampage, hurting others and themselves, blood streaming out from the youngster's forehead, silently sitting near Superdrugs store, the shutters are down and the lights are out, no one's out, no one's alive, they are tormenting the dead. There are many dead demons searching the stores, a few have scorched the front of another well-known store, a few young men have just run out of a clothes shop with jeans under their wings, no doubt a good deal for them but not so for the person they have just stolen from. If only it could have been a scene from Robin Hood, robbing the rich to feed the poor, but the youngsters are flowing quickly like small mosquitos in thin air. I stood still near Oxford Circus tube station for the last hour almost in a daze, watching life go by like a faded blur. A few mobs moving in every direction but most of them going in one direction which spells the commotion of this rioting. The lifeless are being chased by the vulnerable, who are being chased after almost like a tortoise, the young menacing the feeble, the young boy kick the older man just because he can, the tortoises are chased by the hares, the police and in between all these are the lions, the kings of the jungle who rule this area for now at least and down below I can hear the train go by, life is going by but I am standing still.

The masked man, I think he is a man because of his body shape, is hiding behind his handkerchief so that no one can pinpoint who he is but he does have terror streaming through his eyes and I think that his eyes show the same terror that my eyes have, of the unknown, scared of getting attacked, being hurt emotionally or hurting someone else. A lunatic running wild but I am still standing so very still, both of us have something in common. What is he doing here, I don't know, but what am I doing here, I don't know either.

There is a lot of fighting going on, destruction everywhere, but I don't notice so much of that, I see what lies beneath all this chaos, the lovely woman has been pushed to the kerb as she rests her broken faith in the Lord by kissing the cross around her neck, her hair you can tell has been roughened up by the monstrous activity and she shows her age, the silver hair, tossed in a heap like a flat bun. She was in the wrong place at the wrong time and so was her boxed-style handbag, two hard sides, a short thick strap to be held in the hand and all her previous sentimental vanity goods stored within that and kept tightly hidden by two big shiny silver buttons that would cross when needed to be opened. She fumbles to try and get her restored dignity back but alas, she tumbles down again into the exact position. She looks around and opens her mouth to ask for help but utters no words, the fear worsens in her eyes as she puts her trembling right hand to her mouth. She is scared of someone seeing her or hearing her, everyone is too busy to care about her. Her nose streams out clear fluid and as it drips onto her big luscious dark lips, she brushes the liquid dry with her right arm and slowly but attentively looks at the fluid on her sleeve now. Her eyes widen at what she has seen. I presume it was blood as she seemed to have been hurt quite badly, she reaches for her handbag and recklessly forces it open and takes out her mirror in a hope for it to lie to her and tell her that everything is okay. Her face has sunk even though it is still sunny and warm, that sullen grey pale look on her face tells her story of disappointment, but she's not the only one. I call out to her "Mercy, mercy." She doesn't look my way. She looks like a "Mercy" to me, she looks like a friend of mine, who is called "Mercy" so that's why I called her by that name.

There are a lot of people running past Mercy now and I cannot see her any more but I hope she is okay. My eyes search for her, wandering everywhere and my ears are eagerly waiting for her "Yes, I'm alright, I am Mercy and I am alright, the Lord has saved me." But I hear and say nothing. "You ar righ' Ducks?" came a calm voice, but Mercy would not talk like that. She would talk proper English and once again, I hear the same message, this time I could sense it near my legs. An old man, rough and rugged, has come slowly right next to me without me knowing and made his home by my feet. I say home because I was still standing and he was happily sitting enjoying the scene. I think he was "a one-trick pony" because he didn't say anything else except those four words, again and again. He had everything he owned in his big coat pockets as he had things toppling out of them but he couldn't care less. He has a companion with him, his drink cans, he was happy, drinking sip by sip. The fluid kept him happy and listened to what he was saying without upsetting him, a real companion, a man and his drink.

I know that I had not been attacked but did feel pain on my left elbow. I looked at the small but bloody graze and then I looked at the wall where I had been standing for such a long time. There was a small speck of blood smeared on the red brick, faint and flawless. I put my arm down from the cross-armed position and let it dry. I caught sight of that happy man from the corner of my left eye, trying all the while to avoid his gaze but he was still watching me. He smiled, my face squinted and then he quickly winked.

Somehow that seemed to make him so happy, his smile continued and so did my squint. He didn't care that I was angry, not as him, but at his actions, but he was innocent and his companion was not. "You ar righ' Gazza" I said with a nod. He nodded back, even though he probably wasn't Gary or Gazza, but he didn't give a damn.

By this time, the police had moved people away from the scene and everyone seemed to be moving on a bit further down the street and finally the kerb where Mercy was lying was visible again. My eyes searched for her like the busy bee trying to dodge all the mosquitos to find its honey, but Mercy was not there at all. Where was she, she must have got trampled on, but where was she? Her dignity, pride and body had all vanished. I looked in the opposite direction to that of all the people and I slowly took the long walk home, my back towards the lessening noise of people and my front towards normality, the roaring of the cars, silent changing traffic highs and ordinary people getting on with their evening.

Already half an hour of walking and the sky still glowing like a golden field of corn, vibrant and colourful. The smell of diesel and petrol overpowers the smells of the vain humans who manage to smother on so much perfume that some still smell of it. This is life, beautiful life out here but these people don't seem to be tarnished by the going's on of the day or the evening. Everyone seems to be heading to their final destination, like the golden field of corn, all in their own position in life and each and every one an individual. Mercy stood out from the crowd and I am still mesmerized by her disappearance, an unsolved mystery, it's in my head and as a car goes by, it jolted my memory of her again, almost to the point where the roar or the horn of the cars, lorries and truck and the night coaches and the bright red buses resembling and reminding me of the red on her face and blood-stained sleeve. I can see the buses go by, but not Mercy. She's in my head but Gazza is still living in my heart, why?

His body odour is still lingering around my mouth and within my nose and I open and close my mouth and swallow my spit so that his odour will go, but it hasn't. I can feel his unwashed body, his grizzly hair and his rugged, old and tatty urine-impregnated clothes embedded underneath the layers of my skin. His smile and those words that he uttered so happily, a bit like my father. My father, I could say, seemed to be a cleaner and well-groomed version of Gazza and Mercy, a figure of my own mother sitting on the outside of life, waiting to be invited in. Where is she now, where is her "outside" and how will I know where she is? I spoke to Gazza, I spoke to my father today, I called out to Mercy, she didn't hear or reply, that's how it is with my mother. Are you both dead, my father always says that never mourn the dead, always remember the good times and the good life people have been privileged enough to have had. I try hard to remember my mother and the pain began to gnaw at me almost as if I was now standing in the darkness of the night.

"Lilly Roe, you're all by yourself, I do hope that Anthony has actually walked you home," father commanded, but I just stood still and lifeless, my arm bearing the brunt of the knot in the hard wooden cold edge of the doorframe. I can feel my elbow bleeding again, I narrow it towards my body so that the blood doesn't drip. Father tries to come out but I edge him inside because he is looking for Tony and I have only just remembered that he, once again, left me! Father hastens his pace and just as I close the door behind me, I take a final look outside and even now I can still smell Gazza all the way down from my nose to the guts. I slam the door shut behind me whilst quietly trying to make a quick stride up the stairs to my bedroom.

"Not so fast young lady, get in here first," ordered my father. "Yes, father" was all I could say. I quickly got off the creaky bottom step of the stairs as it slowly cracked and creaked with my weight and then it went silent, just like me, as I finally stood in front of my father, waiting to be summoned and questioned, like the judge and perpetrator, but I was feeling like a victim today.

Chapter 5

"Lilly Roe, don't just stand there, sit down, quickly let's eat whilst we watch the news. The riots have taken place again today, many more areas affected and much more devastation everywhere, look." Quietly, I sat beside him on the soft seat, without even washing my hands and watched my father, whilst he watched the news and served dinner. My plate three quarters full and father's full to the edge, warm and satisfying thick onion gravy oozing at the edge, warm meat pie, the mash smothered in the middle with fresh vibrant whole peas and finger-length slim orange zesty carrots. The plate looked so inviting and invigorating and wholesome but all I could smell was Gazza's body odour.

"Have you already eaten, Lilly Roe?" father quickly asked and without even waiting for a reply he quickly said "praise" and began eating. I didn't say praise or eat, but I watched father. "Have you already eaten?" he asked again. I didn't want to lie, in fact I couldn't lie to father ever, there have been times when I have not spoken rather than lying.

I watched him tuck into his food, the clickety-click of the fork and the soft sawing of the knife, dribbled with gravy and carefully the morsels go into the mouth. Father's teeth crunch onto the metal utensils and I watch him slowly but carefully, slide the fork out and onto the plate again, his glass of wine on his left side, as he always drinks with his left hand. As far back as I can remember, father and mother always had wine with their evening meal, at least a couple of glasses each, but I have never seen them drunk. He is totally focused on the news and he doesn't look at me, even though my eyes are peeled on him. He has finished and so has the news.

"Oh dear Lilly Roe, look at the mess these young people have created and got themselves into. There have been arrests, many injured and hurt and the taxpayer is going to have to pay the bill. There must have been thousands of police everywhere, the taxpayer is paying for the extra policing as well. Oh Lilly Roe, what are young people up to nowadays?" he said in a caring but worried tone.

"I don't know father, it's awful, really awful." My words were emotional but he was too busy to notice. He looked at my plate not at me and offered kind words. "Never mind Lilly Roe, you're obviously not hungry." Slowly he scrapped his feet forward and lifted his gigantic body off the sofa. I put my hand on the squashed seat where he was seated and watched the seat go straight up and then looked straight at father. His eyes didn't meet mine, but his sight met the remains of food on my plate. For a moment, he looked at it, but not at me. He then took the place, went to the bin, and scraped the food off it with the fork I had used, straight into the bin. He lifted his foot off the pedal of the bin and the clackety-clack bin lid sealed the bin tight. I pulled my top down properly almost as if I had just ironed it and slowly went to the sink where father had just piled the washing up. Saucepans half dirty, wine glass half-empty and dinner plates full to the rim with gravy slaughtered all over. I took the Fairy Liquid bottle and squeezed the little boy until he squirted green soapy liquid out and as I looked out of the window unaware of the rest of the world, I moved the tea towel round and round the plates.

My father brought me back to reality, "I think that's clean enough Lilly Roe," he said calmly. I quickly rushed the rest of the washing, whilst father dried and put away.

"Good night father," I said lovingly as I stood at the brunt of the door. He looked straight at me, his pupil spread wide in his eye and then he smiled, that warm-hearted smile and replied, "Good night sweet Lilly Roe."

Next morning as I came down the stairs, I could hear the television was on and even though my ears tried so hard to distance themselves from the terrible rioting news, it was impossible to escape the truth. The only thing that distanced the bad news was the earthy solid fumes of the chestnut mushrooms sizzling on the red hot stove, the crackling of the eggs, splattering out the juicy fat. But my stomach could not face the food this morning either. My father acknowledge me but carried on with his chores along with the whistling but did manage to pull out the chair for me to sit on, like a true gentlemen, whilst happily he carried on.

I sat at the table and poured the tea from the freshly-brewed teapot slowly and precisely, trying so hard not to leave a tea-stain streak all the way down the spout. Father put the breakfast on the plates and sat down beside me. He took his left warm hand and put it over my right hand whilst putting his right cold hand onto the cold plateless serving mat which mother often used and then said a prayer. I could hardly hear his prayer but I could feel his hand's warmth and the blood gushing up and down from his fingers as he spoke and then it all stopped.

"Tuck in, Lilly Roe," gently giving me the order to start eating. I could hardly eat anything but I didn't want his effort to go to waste, so I ate the dribbly wet soggy part of the egg on a bit of buttered crunchy toast. I put my knife and fork down and father looked from the corner of his left eye and turned his head to the side, a sign to say "You finished?" I nodded. He took my plate of food and emptied it into his own plate whilst telling me that it will keep him going for a while.

"Father, I wanted to talk to you about mother." He gently put his knife and fork down onto the plate and from the corner of his eye, a stern look followed. "Yes, it's disastrous, isn't it Lilly Roe, how two nights in a row, the trouble these monstrous kids have caused…." He continued but his words were harsh, not concerned, his look was stern not worried, his facial expression was angry and not caring, his lips twitched a little with nervous convictions but he had tenacity in his eyes rather than the serene picture of the sky. His nose stood so very still but it looked as if he was smelling the sounds of anger within him but without saying a thing, his throat swallowed his own spit with some difficulty, his Adam's apple forced itself up and then slowly slid down the back into place as father uttered his final word.

I wonder what happened to Mother Mercy yesterday? Did she get up, did my mother manage to get her life up and running without father and I? There are so many questions about mother that I will never have the answers for. The only thing I was ever sure about was that she was and is my mother but she has left us both. It's not the end of our lives because we love each other very much as well and that's not a consolation prize either, but there isn't a day that goes by when I don't think about her and I know that father feels the same but will never admit it to me. And then there's the radio that's blurting out facts and figures of the chaos and the television, showing pictures and live footage of the aftermath. Everything in life at the moment seems to be like a blank light canvas with lashing of paint thrown in all directions, creating colour and patterns for all to see and interpret what they like, something great or just a mess.

I rose from my seat and touched the seat where he sat, so close to me, but it was not warm anymore, nor was he, he was cool, so unlike him, but the fact that he sat there was reason enough for my senses to stay awake and still love him, in spite of everything. There was only us two now and I had to stick with him. I went straight to him and now he was standing at the sink, his stomach touched the sink, his legs close to the drawers and slowly he stood struggling to get the gloves on, pulling the rubber glove whilst gently trying to ease his finger forward. He wasn't comfortable and it was so clear to see. The tap slowly dripping into the bowl, the washing up liquid twirling round and round whilst the suds slowly rose higher as I looked up at his face, his glance didn't meet mine at all.

"I'll do the washing father," I said, almost like a whisper. He didn't reply but seemed relieved and almost as if he was about to snap, his body came to a halt. His legs moved away from the sink, his hands half in and half out of the gloves, he pauses and then he placed his hands onto the sink. He stands motionless but with the weight of the world on his shoulders.

"I'll make a fresh pot of tea father, please sit down." He didn't utter a word, his eyes didn't stray, even his hair remained combed so perfectly, unmoved and untouched. Whenever he finishes washing, he always smothers his left hand from the right, creating his normal parting, and with only one single movement, he brings his hand all the way down to the nape of his neck and whilst he cannot see, a silver strand of hair always covers his shirt. The hair on his neck, silver, not white, shines effortlessly, short soft whiskers, plentiful.

That day had slowly drifted away but left a tainted smell of our very little conversation, how naïve had I been, the third and fourth day of the riots, not just London but other cities as well - Bristol, Manchester, Birmingham, Liverpool and the list goes on. "Copycat" violence creating havoc and monstrous injuries to innocent people.

David Cameron, the Prime Minister, came back from his holidays to Parliament for an emergency debate on the activities and the state of the country. The newscaster's face normally always looks glum and these days, there was no exception. The numerous reporters doing their job in their own style, informing the public how thousands of yobs were arrested and a thousand of those were charged and millions of properties was damaged.

Civil disorder starting in North London with reflections of muggings, arson, assault and murders, all for justice? Petrol bombs creating fear by the masked mobs and then there's the hand of the law, not so strong, not as visible and powerless. The firefighters risking their own lives for others, coming to the aid of shopkeepers, residential flats and houses. How can the death of one ordinary citizen create such a big bang, a blast whose lava and ash could be seen by most, the tremor of the eruption of events affecting so many victims? I was a victim, lured into insanity by Anthony who I have not seen nor heard from since, but then it's nearly September now and college has finished and I will be starting university next month, a world yet to be explored but without Anthony and without knowing anything else about the train in the night.

Chapter 6

That was August and now it's September. The Notting Hill Carnival has come and serenaded us with all its glamour. The Bank Holiday weekend enjoyed by so many, the noise, music, costumes and of course Jerk chicken, plentiful and aromatic, sweet-like warm fluffy honey, spicy like Big Mamma's curry of authentic Madrassi smells, always tasty and tantalizing even though I was never hungry for it. I remember when my mother took me to see the carnival, but always fed me before we left home, purely because she always said that food on stalls was not of the highest quality and it was fast food, but why did we even go to the carnival? "Food made quickly," she said, "wasn't good" but then she left on the night train and aren't trains quick, yes, those who travel during the day like me and father but the night trains slowly slither along leaving a slime of a trail and lives destroyed in the meantime, that's her. Fast was good for her but not for us!

The arrival of September and it's very much like summer. Still, days of soothing sunshine, the sun's rays brighten the yellow flowers on my bedroom curtain and the blue dot on the big horizon reminds me always of the blue sky, how delightful that really is. The sunshine dancing around the blue horizon. My father always said that I was his little sunshine but now I just didn't feel that I was amongst the bright blue horizon anymore, I was living in the grey. But why now, why not when she left? It's almost as if I had just woken up from that night when she did leave in search of that "night train" that she was longing for, but of course my life didn't shatter until the next morning. It's been over a year but I've woken up.

September days long and sunny, still warm in the mornings and late in the evenings and yet I don't know why I am remembering that month now. Thinking about it carefully, I remember it has been over a year now, but why now? The London riots, and Mercy in particular, but why am I almost haunted by Mercy, I don't know her but I knew my mother and yet I felt Mercy's pain within my bones, cracking with agony and yet the pain was enjoyable too. I think it just made me feel that pain was normal and yet what was happening was not. I never did feel my mother's pain, all these years, I never knew that she ached.

Thinking about it now, why have I thought about Mercy every day since the riots, am I trying too hard to feel my mother's pain and not Mercy's at all and anyway Mercy was no one to me but my mother was nearly everything to me apart from my father. I was much closer to my father even then but since her runaway departure at no particular terminal or to her desired destination, it was strange but somehow we lived as parent and child but we were worlds apart, the ocean had come between our worlds and we weren't good swimmers, just ripples in the waves.

August was not a good month really as many disillusioned and unanswered reflections appeared in our lives and father had seen the changes in me as well. He never said words of disapproval but his face showed what he never uttered. It was as if the London Bridge we both lived on was beginning to crack from the middle and I felt that every crack takes its shudder and father felt its wrath. We still never uttered a word, we were obedient and lived in a civilized manner.

September was a very reflective month and it was as if time had stood still and we were both the remainder's of our family life, not part of it, both of us with the painted wide lips showing a crack of a half-smile, no loud noises of laughter even when "Only Fools and Horses" was on, the television laughed but we the audience did not. Our words to each other were always comfortable before but now they were just polite. The armchair started to lose that saggy feeling in the middle of the seat and the ripples, almost like water, on the arms of the soft chairs were straightening themselves out. Our home was slowly becoming a house, all the four walls were still there but the bricks were showing signs of movement, the carpet was still clean and yet the tainted smell of life was aromatic. His left hand that shook ever so slightly slowed vengeance on his face, until then she always held his right hand between hers and slowly, with reassuring warm eyes, she stared into his, the demons on his face would lift as she placed his right hand on his left. He didn't have a care in the world and yet he still fingered the cracks in his palm.

October has begun and it's almost as if I have lost a month of my life, Father and I still in the same house but not so comfortable with one another, we only really exchanged civilized conversation like "Hello and how are you?" He continued to cook whilst keeping his head down and now not even peeping from the corner of his eye. We sat and watched the television together but only commented on the programme rather than us, we laughed at the comical side of others' lives especially those aired on Radio Four but we couldn't even air ours let alone laugh or cry. How did we get here, from a happy family of three to a father and daughter living in the same house but alone. Its bedtime for those who crave sleep but for me my body's tired and my mind's exhausted but I'm not asleep.

A slow, almost silent hum creeps slowly out of the clock and then I hear struggling of the big hand pacing itself and then there is pure silence. For a second, it's blissful and then suddenly it starts singing. I open my left eye slightly as my lashes cover my half-open eye, my hand slowly braves the cold and I place it on the clock. My eyelash is curled and poking into my pupil. I will cut it off today. I blink both of my eyes, it feels better now and the man has started to read the news on the radio. The clock beeps, the music starts, Capital Radio, so nice, lively songs unlike my life and sleeptime and then the newsman reading off his scuffled paper the miserable news, always miserable, but at least the weather is good so he says, but then how does he know at six o'clock in the morning. He's guessing, I know.

I lay in bed silently and slowly gather the sheet on the mattress underneath me from where it was creased by my feather weight. I could feel the dust, the curled up hair and the small parcels of stony dirt from my body that have gathered on my sheet, day after day. It's strange but I do make my bed everyday so to remove any DNA that I may have left whilst sleeping, but no matter what, it's always still never perfectly clean or uncreased except the first night after it's been washed. This is only since a year now, not before that because mother used to make the bed then, some people cannot do chores forever.

Slowly I manage to get out of bed when the man says "it's six-thirty and let's catch up with…." I head straight for the big mirror beside my bed. I look into it rather than at it, I peer at myself, my curly locks straggling around my neck, I pull the big lock on my eye to straighten it but it's spring was still tight. Perhaps I should put gel on it or my spit. I try and move it away from my eye by blowing from the corner of my lips. I am still staring at the young, vulnerable and fragile kid in front of me, my right hand is still pulling my nightie down. I like it on my knees but it's always above my knees and at least when I am in bed, it's on my knees. I like my skirts on my knees as well and my dresses, but most of mine are over my knees. Mothers were always exactly on the knee but I never saw her pull hers down.

I don't even realize but now I have noticed that the girl in front of me is plastering her curly hair on her forehead, keeping her parting to the left and whilst using her left hand. I didn't even realize that I can smell her left hand, it smells sweaty and stale, I wonder why? Do my hands smell like that as well, no they don't because why should they, my mother's hand always smell of perfumed cream and mine do too! Some taint the natural smell and I don't.

I notice how the night dress is clinging under the left breast tightly. Are my breasts deformed or what, why do they look different shapes and now from my blurry vision I can see the left one quite clearly, it's much darker than the right, one is of a brown girl and the other of a white girl. Maybe not a lot and I keep my eyes, that's both of them, tightly on my tit. "Oh no!" I blurt out, I can't even talk to Father about this, I really can't because girls talk to mums about private things, not dads. I wouldn't expect father to talk to me about his bit, no. The nightdress is damp where the crease has been hiding. I can see that girl in front of me yawning, her big massive teeth snarling at me, her miserable temperament turning into something like a lioness's roar and her brows narrow as if she's in pain.

"It's seven o'clock and this is the news...." I pull the nightie right down now, the crease is shadowed a little but all of a sudden, the nightie is equal and my breasts are what they should be and that bad-tempered, miserable girl seems fine now as she narrows her hands towards the pink gown hanging on the cold smoky hook. Pink, fluffy and warm hugging a cold unloved dark mysterious hook, always hidden, what has it got to hide, what does the night train have to hide?

October chilly morning and as always my father has opened the window a little to let the smell of the breakfast eggs snapping away on a faraway carriage, out to breathe the fresh air. I push the kitchen door wide open and father as always gently says "Morning Lilly Roe." There's a cold feel to his warm mouth as he no longer says "Good morning," it's just "morning" now. The cold man stands beside the warm gas cooker, his heart and eyes, both warm but not mellow, his tongue calm and yet his words in jeopardy. His eyes deliberately don't meet mine as Father serves the breakfast on hot plates that he has forgotten to place under the grill to heat, hot breakfast on a hot plate. It fills my stomach but not my heart, but some eat to fill their tummies and others to fill their hearts.

After breakfast, I grab my bag and coat and reach for my father's weak arm and for the first time in over a month, he actually realizes that I am standing next to him. His legs start to shudder inside his quivering trousers with a perfectly pressed line in the middle, how strange, our life's not perfect but his trousers are. I take his right strong hand and mine is almost invisible in his and slowly my eyes follow my action. Just like Mother, I place his right hand over his left and he presses them onto his stomach. I wait and wait, for what, I don't know, I really don't know, but I keep looking straight at his eyes. I wait and wait and then in the deep, deep silence, he lifts his eyes and stares straight into mine. His eyes are wet like the sea and mine like the cold dripping tap, drip drip.

That day, that autumn October

morning was a breakthrough, at least Father looked at me again, that was good. We breathed the words to console each other but our tears understood it all. That deep silence was golden, almost as if the crop was plentiful but without having anything to harvest, a field full and yet, worthless. Tears, priceless, and there were plenty of those for the first time ever that I saw, like the stream that has yet to merge into the lake. He stood still and silent but I hear that little child inside of me, the one who stared at me in the mirror that morning calling out for that train to come back. Whenever I am asleep I can hear that train whisking people along the journey and yet, during the day and that morning, I saw the night train puffing along but it was silent, like death and yet I saw the corpses alive, laying waiting for their coffins.

Time had no bearing that day as we

both stood still for such a long time and then I could see the red light of the cooker flashing timidly as always, bleeping without much life, it showed me that it was half past eight. My father's hands were almost clasped together and I directed him towards the armchair, he didn't sit in his own but sat in hers instead. His buttocks fitted snuggly into the moulded shape of hers and then I gently wiped his tears with my left hand and remembered that it didn't smell pleasant and so with the right hand I finished wiping his tears. He kept looking at the floor, at my feet and the black smelly leather. I bent over and kissed him on his right cheek.

There was no response from him, no broken silence only dumb silence, his tears rolled but his face didn't quiver, his lips didn't warm to return any words and his eyes, as he looked to see me leave, they looked like barren motherland with no life on it, empty scrubland, hopeless. My throat dry and almost choking as if the words were entangled within but there was no escape, my lips covered with thick shiny lip gloss and then there was a thin salty line sliming itself down from the corner, it dribbled into my mouth and slowly I lifted my bottom lip to let it seep into my mouth. "Bye Father" is all I could manage. Politely, he nodded and then just before I closed the door on my back, I reminded him that I was going to uni and will be back a four o'clock. He showed no interest in what I had said and yet he registered it all, he didn't shake his head as he would normally, instead he lifted his index finger of his right hand and waved it up and down as if to say that "it's okay". He didn't shake his head or lose his dignity.

All day long I was at uni and even though I was busy, really I should have been focusing on that but instead, all I could think and remember was the way he could not look up at me, through the lack of dignity, respect, pride or pain, yes pain, real pain. The kind of pain that has no words, you see it all so clearly, it's a canvas which has a clearly-painted picture where different times show different emotions. The pain was choking him and so much so that he couldn't utter a word and so his finger did the speaking. "What would he be doing?" was on my mind as if those few words were scratched on my forehead, so I couldn't forget even if I wanted to.

It was an easy first day at the university and after getting our timetables, meeting new students and staff and sharp taster lessons and of course in between that there were chances of getting coffees, muffins, lunch and coffees again. Somehow today even the coffee tasted bitter and whilst others commented on how good it was, all I could say was how bitter life tasted. I left university at two o'clock and was home before the school rush hour, way before the office crowd made their way home. I say "office crowd" because we live in the South of England, in North London in a small town near the River Thames. There are lots of offices here and cafes, bars and restaurants and from our small house, it's only a few minutes walk into the hustle bustle of busy life and yet we are far enough away from it as well. It's always been a nice place to live, the house, the road and the town.

At three o'clock, I touch the big cold brass knocker of the front door and it hits hard against its head. There is silence inside and my eyes sway from side to side and my ears alternatively open themselves wide to take in the noise and life of the great outdoors, it's silent outdoors as well. In anticipation, I keep imagining that

Father's hair will shine through the stained glass of the front door and then as he gently fiddles with the lock, before he gently slides the door ajar whilst moving his own body with the movement of the door, but it didn't happen today. I peer through the letterbox, "Father, father," the words come echoing back on my cheeks and then my hair moves as if the memory of the words blow a gentle gust through my locks. It almost seems like a scene from the film "Scream" but there is no one who is going to come and get me, and strangely enough it puts a lot of questions through my tiny mind.

Why am I knocking and why do I always do this when in reality I have a door key? It's not because I don't want to use it or cannot but because it feels great when Father walks down the hall, his hair shimmering against the glass door and above all, he comes and welcomes me in. It's not even what he says but the way he says "Come on in, Lilly Roe, hope you had a good day." Father's favourite flowers are lilies, the strong scented lilies, no matter what colour and mine are the same. I like colourful lilies, preferably not just white as they resemble death, and I do love sunflowers, colourful vases full of lilies and sunflowers. Every Friday when Mother used to go shopping, she would always buy a bunch of lilies and sunflowers because she liked sunflowers and even though they were always two tiny bunches, when the lilies opened up, the vase became full and scented. The sunflowers resembled many moods of the people in this house, small bunch as we are a small family and I always use to sit at the bottom of the stairs and reflect on the smells and the colours. The colours always amaze me and I don't know why but it was a habit, I suppose, after I had looked at the vase for long enough without even seeing the vase itself, I always went upstairs to slowly to open my wardrobe and stare at the different colours arranged in it, just like the vase. Is this why Father named me Lilly, but then where did the Roe come from?

I take out my unused key, one thing I never leave home without and you know my door key was given to me when I reached the age of twelve, my first day at school, big secondary grammar school, by my father. I remember that first day because I felt so special. I had grown up and I was going to grammar and not comprehensive school. Father said that grammar was always for those who wanted to study well and get on in life and he went to grammar as well. He uttered these wise words and kissed me on my forehead and then took me to the front door whilst Mother watched on. Then he stood still and put his right hand into his perfectly pressed black trousers. I still remember the crease edging its head away a little from the remainder of the trouser leg and then he grinned. I watched his hand, waiting for an unexpected gift but I kept an eagle eye on his face as well. The lines on his forehead oozed out a little sweat and the corner of his left side of the mouth grew wider, a tiny clear clean smile, it made me even more eager to get my present. Suddenly this shiny, silver clean and unused metal key was handed to me by Father. It was cold but bore all the intentions of me being a grown-up now, someone who was responsible and I intended on living up to expectations, but just the key, I was not expecting.

All that hype and drama about the door key was so dramatised but father believed in making the most of small things in life and a lot of things were ceremonial in our life but then Mother thought they were all trivial. As the ceremonies took place, Mother would look on and silently shake her head. Whilst taking the key from his hand and unlike a lady or grown-up, I quietly slipped it into my bra so the story of the unused key began. I would put it into my bra when I left home and when I get back I always go straight to my bedroom, take the key out and get changed and finally come into the sitting room. That was a routine, but then that was learnt by Father and Mother.

"What else have you got in your pocket for me, Father?" was all I asked. He shook his head and replied, "The key is all I have for you Lilly Roe, really, that's it, now off you go and enjoy the day." His smile remained on his face but he could tell that I was a bit disappointed. He could recognise that look, it wasn't the eyes or the forehead but whenever I was upset a line of disappointment slid across right next to my left eyebrow, near the middle. He knew that look and understood it well without me even uttering a word.

"Father, are you home?" There was no reply and I could sense that he had been gone for a very long time now. There was no lingering of nutty burnt smoke smell or the lingering of sweet honey-worn carpet smell where his feet roamed. There were no smells, it was cold and yet the house was warm enough, there were smells but I couldn't smell anything. I touched and held my key and then slid it back into its safe place. With the back of my shoe heel, my foot closed the worn out door shut. The front door always looked worn out from the bottom because we all had a habit of slamming or kicking the door shut. Throughout its life with us, it had suffered and lived an eventful life. It bore the brunt of our moods. As I scraped my knee against the bannister rail, I slowly touched the top base of it as this is where Father lays his hand, his right hand, and then puts it into his coat or trouser pocket and then leaves home.

As I entered my room, I noticed that everything was as I had left it in the morning. I kicked off my shoes near the entrance of my door, one facing the north and the other to the west and slowly slumped myself on my red flowered duvet whilst resting my bum on the red flower listening to the silence. I love this moment and since Mother left, there have been so many times like these. I sensed within me this same feeling when I paraded the red duvet, with a collection of red sunflowers spread out in the middle but then the flowers were no longer in the vase in the hall anymore. For some weird reason that I cannot understand, why am I focusing on flowers, sunflowers on my bed don't have smell and nor does the house, and I am thinking that maybe the house only smells when humans live in it and humans only smell when they are alive. The house is alive with people in it and that's why my hand didn't smell nice this morning, but I won't smell it now.

I shouldn't think about it, I should do it and that is to wash my hands regularly with soap, but I did use the lavatory at university and only rinsed my fingers without even using soap. Mercy, that Lady, seemed an awfully nice lady, she had a red poppy-like flower on her dress. Blood red lipstick. Mother always wore it. I hear the key in the door, I get up, get the red blood lipstick and quickly smother it from left to right across my lips and then sit at the top of the stairs. It's ten to four and my father has walked in, head down and dampened eyes just like this morning.

Chapter 7

I pretended not to notice him and he did the same, so he didn't get a chance to see my red blood lipstick and the lack of skills in wearing it with required etiquette or applying it professionally, well I don't often wear it, I prefer lip gloss so even if it slips off the lips, no one notices. Like a creepy crawly I remove myself from the stairs into my room and I stand once again in front of that beloved Magic Mirror. It's the only thing that can tell me the truth without hurting or upsetting and without even uttering a word.

That girl in front of me is looking straight into my eyes, she seems to be withdrawn from life but when I look at her lips, she looks very much alive. That red lipstick on her lips is making me frustrated, but why? I ignore her and as my hand quickly reaches my wardrobe door, I notice gunk in my tiny finger of my left hand. Should really wash my hands often! I tuck the dirty finger into my palm, there, no one will notice and anyway, no one is here. I pull off a red cashmere v-neck sweater and change into it and hunt for what would go with it, black jogging bottoms, perfect.

"Don't creep around Lilly Roe, come inside, I've made a pot of tea, Yorkshire tea, our favourite." I didn't know that he had heard me coming towards the door as I quietly looked through the crack of the open door. I went in and walked towards where he was sitting whilst he poured tasteful tea for me. "Why Lilly Roe, is this a new way of wearing lipstick?"

"Father?" I blurted. "How do you know I am wearing lipstick? You didn't even look at me!"

Without making it obvious he wiped his weeping eyes with his jersey-emerald top and then looked straight at my lips, not my eyes. "Do you think that I don't notice girl, a father has eyes at the back of his head for his child and really Lilly Roe, what the hell, is it fashion or what to wear it this way?" There seemed to be a glint in his eyes whilst saying that and suddenly without even thinking about it, we both started laughing. He was laughing at my lipstick and I was laughing to see him laugh.

"Why are you crying Lilly Roe, just

now we were both laughing and now the tears, why Lilly Roe, talk to me." Sitting there next to him, still holding my tea cup with the saucer rattling in my hand I gently reply, "If you have eyes at the back of your head then you'll know that it's also nice for you to look at me, which you don't now, why Father?"

"Drink your tea now dear and don't cry and anyway you said you'd be back at four. When did you get in and when did you put the lipstick on, anyway?" He slowly puts the weight of his shoulders on his right hand and tries to push himself up from the sofa but I quickly hold his arm and pull it down for him to sit down.

"Anyway Father, let's talk, I need to talk but more so you, you need to talk. Father don't look away, this is killing me!" I hate talking to Father like this but I have no choice as he slowly starts to look at me again, now he was wearing that frowned criss-cross look on his forehead. He was upset. I told him that I came home just before three and all he kept saying was "Why did I come home early?"

"Forget about me coming home early, forget about my lipstick, forget about uni, forget about tea, let's talk about Mother. I've been waiting to talk about her for over a year and deep down inside you want to, but you always find it easier to ignore rather than solving the problems, unlike Mother." There was silence once again, the heat from my anger and his body heat radiating out of his sweater, his palms became sweaty and I take a deep breath, I can smell the sweat on his palms. He quickly rubs them together, the sound of a fine sandpaper rubbing together, he has hardworking hands. He worked all those years on the railway and brought home a lot of money for Mother and only stopped working when she said to him that the money he brings home doesn't pay for her extras anymore. He asked her why it wasn't enough anymore but was before, to which she replied, "It just isn't!" They didn't know I heard this, I was sitting on my bed, with the door open and they were quarrelling downstairs. It was past my bedtime so they assumed I was asleep and then I think he hit the nail on the head, he told her that he had noticed a change in her, her going out, staying out till late and singing under her breath about the night train during the day and in the bathtub singing with the water pattering away. He told her that she didn't love him anymore and was seeing someone else.

And then there was a chill that feathered softly on my back and it's as if my back was colder than normal and that was over two years ago, but since then and soon after that he became agitated and then we both noticed the obvious. His left hand had started to shake a lot of the time and it was getting weaker as well and all Mother could do was to put the good hand over the left. With this he was not fit for work anymore even though he had five years left before pension, but they gave him some money as a goodbye package.

Mother seemed happy with the package and a few months later, the package probably brought her ticket for the singing night train. The months that led up to the night train rattling our life, there was a strange silence between them. First there was great tranquillity, then the odd rows and after one row, everything was silent. That night, I remember it well, it was my birthday, 23rd August 2011 and we had a family celebration and Father brought us a mobile phone each and Mother, who never worked in her life, not much at home either as Father was the main house provider and house husband as well, brought me a laptop which I still have. I think she brought me my goodbye package, just like Father's.

In the morning, 24th August, my birthday became a distant memory as she rekindled that unlit flame of hers and as for my birthday, that was the last time it was celebrated. Father was silent for that day but the following morning he was back to his normal self. Our life was normal except for her absence. Father and I were still good together and it wasn't until the London riots that we have drifted apart. If I hadn't been so foolish, then at least Father and I would have been good and now we are both sitting next to each other trying to talk about our life without Mother but being unable to. I went to the Notting Hill Carnival the year before but that year it was 2010.

In fact last year, I didn't really remember it because there was enough silent commotion at home.

Quietly and silently I offer my father my hand and he puts his right hand onto the palm of my hand. He is looking straight at me but somehow I cannot see, but can sense that he is looking at his shaking left hand, within himself he is very much aware of it shaking. I get up and slowly go and sit on his left side now, he smiles and his face changes from almost being ashamed to being uneasy, the corner of his bottom lip twitching against his big rugged teeth, not all even but strong, big and manly. I now put my left hand palm onto his lap and take his left hand and place it onto mine. He smiles, a happy content smile, wide, not just his smile but his eyes are smiling as well, a stubborn mule who won't go to the doctor for his shakes. All in good time though because one day when the time is right for him, he will have to face up to his illness, either when he gets worse and can't cope or maybe when she's back, as she can convince him to think her way and to keep the peace, he'll listen.

He takes a long pause, a long sigh to gather his memories and thoughts and then just as when I thought that he is going to talk, he reassuringly puts his other hand on mine and we clasp our hands together snuggly like a staple. I can feel his warm hand soothing my inner body, the tingling sensation, his blood moving around his hands reaching within my own hands, warming my arms, so soothing almost as if I didn't need to hear anything at all but today I had to, for his sake, not mine. A bit of the red lipstick is smothered over my fingers and I can still see the tiny nail with the black gunk stuck inside but I choose to ignore it, after all Father is not going to notice or tell me to go and wash my hands first, like she always did, but never mocking, no, my parents never mocked me.

I look away from my hand and look directly into his eyes, the mysterious sea to be explored by someone adventurous but did I really want to explore the truth, yes I did, I needed to. He looks at me and slowly tries to look away. I shake my head, he looks back at me, his eyes are saying so much and without him uttering a word but his heart racing towards that damn train, I can feel his pain and humiliation deep down in my aching heart but my head was not consoled with this, so I gently ask "Father, please tell me, we're in this together."

For the next three hours, he talked mainly and I listened. Everything he said, I agreed with and yet he didn't say anything against Mother either. He talked about the fact that my mother was always looking for something else and someone else who could fill that gap of that something that she was in search of but she didn't know herself what that was but was convinced that there's got to be more to life than she had with Father. Once his hand started to shake, he was slowly losing his dignity but instead of showing and having empathy for her husband, she offered sympathy which he would brush off because it empowered her and make him feel worthless. They were no longer being a husband and wife anymore, even though they shared the same bed and same room and the rift was irreplaceable when she told him in a row that he was no longer the man she married. He asked her if she still loved him and she said she did but he was not man enough for her and so her search continued whilst is pain deepened. Father said this was the breaking point for him because he was a male but not man enough?

Father said that she didn't tell him when she left so he only knew when he awoke in the morning and he was convinced that she did have someone else who promised her that he will take her away from this dull life of hers for an exciting new life with him and she was convinced that a new life, a new man was definitely a better new way of life for her. He said that she only wanted excitement from her life with father and father was stable, steady, assertive, kind and the most excitement that you could get out of father was either watching football on television or playing golf with his mates who always peered over the top of newspapers. He was always happy to go for long weekends, short breaks, camping in the valleys and family run-around games and in the evenings he was happy to go out for a meal, a real restaurant with real food and stay at home and play cards, dominoes or chess, and some of us only play draughts.

He said that any of that and all of that needed money and he never said "no" to what he had. She could spend it how she liked, he didn't question her for he always said that his money is for his family but she always wanted long cruises, foreign tours, long drives through the canyons and jeep rides through the barren deserts with belly dancers for entertainment. Instead of going to a park for a picnic and Father always packed the picnic, she preferred a taxi ride to wine and dine in Harrods, the Savoy and the Ritz but my father was not interested in that and he always said to her that she was free to go and on many occasions she did and I think that it all started to go wrong from there after all, too much of a good time cannot be good for anyone.

Chapter 8

It was half past seven and even I didn't actually feel like eating, my stomach was rumbling and his was as well. Father did most of the talking and it was as if the weight was lifted from his burdened shoulders. The criss-cross worry line seemed to be flatter on his forehead, perhaps it was a relief for us both as there were no tears and there were short bursts of rays of sunshine and it wasn't from the outside either. It was a cloudy day outside and it had been very cloudy in here as well but as the sky darkens outside, the light radiates well inside. I have put the bright lamp on, which always sleeps during the day in the corner beside a model cat who of course sleeps all day long with her eyes open.

Father suggests that we eat as it's important to eat on time but I can tell that he is in no mood to cook which is very unusual for him, he does like to cook and do the washing but is happy for others to tidy up. Thinking aloud I suggest that we should have Heinz beans on toast. Inquisitively, father looks at me and then I quickly say, "You know father, we have not had beans on toast for ages for dinner, let's be different, let's be exciting."

He slowly nods, "Exciting, alright, let's be exciting."

"Exciting like the train" we both whisper together. He puts his right hand on the sofa to balance his weight and yes he does have enough of it, he is a big man, fifteen stones of muscle, over six feet in height and strong except for the one part that sadly shakes now, his own hand and his hand in the shaking of the night train.

We both stand near the gas cooker, I start to open a can of Heinz beans with a can opener that only has half of its teeth and father puts the freshly baked crusty bread into the toaster. He puts it on setting two and when it pops out, he turns it over and lowers the setting to one and a half and lets it brown. It's perfect, four slices of white crusty bread, perfectly brown both sides. He opens the cutlery drawer and takes out the blue-handled knife and with his right hand, he takes the butter from the cereal drawer and it's always Anchor butter and it's in the wrong drawer and tries very hard to spread it on and not sparingly. He cannot manage and so he still doesn't despair but instead tries again, this time he succeeds. He is not tiresome or helpless but maybe just needs a little help at times. The beans are bubbling away in the small pan, I turn the gas off, Father takes two plates out of the cupboard and turns the grill on to warm them, as always.

"Father, there is no need, let's leave that, cold plates are fine, the food's hot, what do you say, less work, live a little." He chuckles and repeats, "Live a little." I plate up and father makes some tea, he puts the small coffee table in front of the sofa. I put the television back on and together we sit and sip our tea without making a noise, Mother used to hate silence but today we watch a movie instead of either the news or politics or, indeed sports. He starts to talk about the move and he is watching and enjoying it even though I was not really watching it at all. He makes   comfortable   relaxed conversation about it, these movies are new to him. He only watched movies with Frank Sinatra, Bob Hope and Betty Davis and some that I've watched with him with Elizabeth Taylor and Rock Hudson. But this movie is a new-age movie, more my age, but he is making an effort, that he didn't before.

The volume of the television set is lowered as I get up to tidy up, he stands next to the sink, picks up the green-coloured scourer and puts plenty of Fairy liquid on it. He starts to scrub the plates, knives and forks whilst I use Dettol kitchen cleaner spray and a tea towel to wipe over surfaces. I can sense that he is listening to the movie still even though he is not watching it, he is busy looking out of the kitchen window, quarter draped at the bottom with a net as he overlooks onto the back. He is miles and miles away but definetly not on the train, in her world,

I have watched him scrub the same plate, his own plate round and round at least twenty times.

"If only we could wipe away or wash away certain bits of our lives Lilly Roe, if only it were that easy!" I didn't say a thing but instead I went and turned the hot water tap on for him, he nodded and started rinsing the perfectly-scrubbed plate. After a couple of minutes, the washing up was done and the kitchen was tidy once again, it had served its two diners well and then father turned the switch off for the kitchen area but the lamp in the dead cat's corner was still alight. The aroma of toast, hot toast with lashings of butter was still alive. Mother always wanted a new big cooker with the six rings and a cooker hood to take away the smell of food but father always said that she hardly ever cooked and he was "Fine with the old one". He was happy with the window open and didn't care if the kitchen still smelt of yesterday's supper and it always did.

As we sat down, I knew he was not going to start talking again and so I asked the burning question, had he tried to contact her or even by accident seen her anywhere? Instead of replying, he started commenting on the movie. I repeated my questions and ignorantly he ignored again, finally I lost my cool and grabbed the remote control and turned the television completely off. I could feel the ever so slight buzz of the lamp purring away and the slow hiss of the fridge in the dark corner near the pantry, but I didn't hear his voice, his nervous cough, his uncomfortable swallowing of his spit down his throat but I hear the answer within my ears so clearly. My head kept throwing the alphabet out into the air for my mind and eyes to read and make sense of it but I had been as thick as planks of wood because I couldn't add up simple numbers, all this time. His silence and no reply to this question was taking us back to the beginning again, his wet eyes in the morning I can understand but why at three-fifty in the afternoon? He knew I was coming back at four o'clock so he got home ten minutes earlier, why is he home most of the time for when I get home, why was he shocked at me coming home early and why, oh God why, were his eyes wet when he came in?

I put my face into my left hand and poured my thoughts into it whilst he looked at the empty walls around us that told so many tales. The paint that never ever got finished, the lamp with the trimming half cut off by Mother in a hope that he will buy another, the half-worn carpet rug where three sets of different-sized feet sat, rubbed and dirtied the area and then there's that 28" inch television, blaring out all of the time and the radio constantly on low volume showing us that it's still alive. Is father a big part of this furniture, is he the furniture, Mother had no control of it did she see herself as a piece of furniture that didn't want to belong in this house, what is their story? Where do I belong in that story?

"Where were you today Father, I know that you are hiding something but I am going to find out. You hadn't been shopping because you had no bags with you, you had been crying when you came home and you were startled to realize that I was home early. If you'd been to see your friends you would not have been crying, you are your happiest with them, so I know you weren't with them. Where were you father and why were you upset? Father, talk to me please, talk to me." I stopped talking but he didn't say anything, that horrible silence buzzing away at me continued and it was as if I didn't know where the button was to turn it off.

"God, Jesus Christ, Father Joseph and Mother Mary, every day, well not today, but most days we say grace and in return all I ask is that you show my father the right path to guidance, he deserves happiness, he's a good man, he was a good husband and is a wonderful father, please Father Joseph reach out to him, the Father, the Son and the Holy Spirit, make my father strong."

At this moment almost as if we are sitting on the beaches of beautiful Bournemouth, as we have done many times and as if the waves have all stopped, how could that be, it could be, to give me that tranquillity and peace to put the pieces together and then I blurted it out, "Father, you went to see Mother today, I know it."

All of a sudden, his left hand started

moving anxiously a bit more than normal, he puts his right hand on his left arm so that the shivering movement may become less and it did but his eyebrow, the right busy eyebrow became arched unlike the one on the left. Then I felt bad but there I was talking to God, the Almighty, Joseph, Mary and Lord Jesus Christ, and then I go and tell fibs.

"I didn't go to uni father, I followed you instead because you were really upset and I felt bad for leaving you on your own and I wanted to know what you were up to." There was still no movement, I really didn't know what else to say as I didn't know anything at all but I blurted out whatever came into head. "I saw you father with Mother." He didn't give me a chance to say anything else, his nostrils were flaring, his eyes both high and eager to explode with what they had heard and the bitterness of the conversation that left a tainted smell, he took a deep breath but I was not scared and he knew it and I had no reason to be either, he never shouted so loudly, swore or hit or threatened even. He always manages to calm himself down all by himself and he always was the one who calmed her fever pitch anger and he always, always apologized. I think Mother took advantage of that, his kind and tolerant nature.

"Well Lilly Roe, if you saw us then there is nothing more to say," calmly he replied. I was more confused than ever.

"I need you to tell me Father, please!" and so he did once he calmed down, the anger and frustration had gone and he admitted that he had been in search for her for a very long time, and with the help of his friends, he finally tracked her down. It's strange how when she left on the night train, she travelled all night with her mystery man and many months later when the London riots took place, she had come back to London from Scotland where she had stayed. It was just a coincidence that one of his friends saw her and told Father that she was right here in London and so the search began and yet it all makes sense now because since then, he had started to get distant from me and all our conversations had ended as well.

After finally tracking her down, he had visited her tiny room which she had rented with a family and he asked Mother to talk to him. She was very unresponsive to him but he kept trying, nearly every day, but somehow the flame at the end of the tunnel just never did get lit, the more he said he tried, the more he felt the distance he was creating with her and the more words he uttered, the greater the pain started becoming. The less he said, the less she looked at him and at times, the only way to talk to her was when he would stand around the corner from where she lived and when she came out, he would try, but he couldn't force her to listen, it was as if her leaving him had meant that she had forgotten that part, that sacred part of their life together. She had asked him not to come back, those were her final words.

Chapter 9

Father repeated, "Not to come back."
These words seem so final, not open-
ended, so that's that then, time to move
on and forget that part of our life, after
all some people want to be found and
others want to be left alone. I think that
it did bring closure to our conversation
and that part of our life and I don't
want father to be belittled anymore and
I think that chapter for us is closed.
"That's that then, Father" is all I could
say and then we both sat and wiped

away our tears, plastered on a smile and got on with life. Father gets up to make his cocoa in milk, two teaspoons full of the delightful powder into the warm milk in a tiny saucepan on that same stove that warmed the beans. He slowly adds a teaspoon of sugar, white crunchy and sweet into his mug and as he stared out of the window, still stirring the sweet delight in his mug, waiting for the white frothy liquid to go dark and mysterious like the dark train with its windows shut to the outside world, he pours it into his mug.

He looked really peaceful and serene when I left him in the kitchen. I go upstairs and after going to the toilet, I contemplate on whether I should use the liquid soap, Radox I think, or Dove bar soap or just be myself and rinse with cold water only, after all, she's not coming to check. As I shut my bedroom door with the back of my foot I unintentionally bring my hands to my nose, they don't smell bad. It's eleven now and I get ready to sleep, my half-shrunk nightie nearly touching my knees, it's a red nightie, so bad things learnt today and I wear my red almost wilted-away nightdress and turn my duvet back to front so that the big red flower is near the pillow. I get into bed and sit not on the bed sheet but on that big red flower. There's a pen and drawing pad on the end of my bed. I kick it off, I laugh and now I am silent.

Now that I have opened my wardrobe and I can see clearly the red teeny weenie bits of clothing, I feel that is all my family but one thing's missing, so I get up again and reach for that red lipstick and smother it from one end of my big mouth to the other corner. Thick shavings of red blood, it eases my pain but then as I close the lid I see a smudge, it's not mine. I put it close to my nose and poke a bit in my nose, to smell it properly, my hand lotion, it's that awful-smelling cocoa butter hand cream, but I never wear it because it stinks and because she bought it for me. I open the hand cream, it has been dipped into and smothered, unlike a virgin as it was before. Father wouldn't use my hand cream or lipstick.

I can see Coco the Clown sitting on that red flower all in red through the mirror, I hate Coco the Clown. I ignore her and start scribbling on the pad, "I hate Mother" again and again and as I look at myself twirling the pen round and round, I think of how many germs are on this page now. Every time I lift my eyes from the writing pad I see the clock has moved even further and the last time when I looked, it was half past twelve, but I can still see the slightly brown girl Coco looking at me, she looks like a brownish golliwog but then I am white, so it's not me, but she looks an awful sight.

Even though all this scribbling was therapeutic, at the back of my head, the bit that hears what the world cannot, I hear the night train chugging away. It is night now and I don't know whether it's a steam train puffing into the distance but I know it's not a modern electric train. I wonder what iron Mother is using now, an electric iron or fathers old heavy coal-fuelled worn-out wartime steam iron, whichever ones it is, who cares?! Every time I put the pen down, the train stops and there are no passengers in my room. I know no one's here but I feel that the invisibles are lurking around, it's two-twenty in the morning, my curtains are still not drawn, the moon with the half-bright smile and that golliwog has just curled over on top of the pad and dozed off, unintentionally but Coco the Clown is not wearing her smile.

"It's Capital Radio, rise and shine, let's go over to the newsroom…. it's coming up to seven o'clock." My legs and arms feel very cold as I realize that I have slept on top of the duvet all night. It's raining and my right hand index finger has arthritic pain, do I have arthritis or was it broken when I was a kid, but the rest don't hurt. I look at it carefully, there's still a tiny smudge of red lipstick inside the nail. Never mind, I might use the Dove soap.

I jump out of bed, grab the writing pad and run straight into Father's bedroom, shouting all the while "Father, Father, Mercy's getting into the night train."

"Oh for heaven's sake, what the hell's happening? What's wrong Lilly Roe, what is it child?"

I went on to explain how Mercy, the woman I saw at the London riots who fell and hurt her pride and even though I only saw her from behind, I know that she's the one who is boarding the night train and it is night as the sky is a grey black, little hope except for the strong beam of the platform light and then Mercy's half-lit face, the other side shadowed by the darkness of the train. It's not that clear but it's almost as I saw her that day, a bit of a blur but I know one thing for sure and that is that her left foot, black shiny and pointed, is on the train, size six I think, and the other foot is still on the platform. She is looking at the life she has just left behind as she boards and I can see other passengers on the train. There is isolation and disillusion surrounding the scene everywhere and especially on Mercy's face, she's not happy. She has this mysterious scarf, black with only one red dot on it covering the shaded part of her face.

The red pen and the black pen and the lined white writing paper, what were they painting for me? I put the three things into my rucksack and fling it over my black coat which I appropriately wore today, it was a dismal grey day today and Father with his half-opened eyes, his silver wig-like hair plastered around his neck and head and he was shocked at what I was saying. It didn't make sense to him nor to me, thinking about it, it was all nonsense, but that wasn't so bad, as something else lingered far more because for the first time in my life I felt the aroma of Father's mouth. I did look at his teeth as he spoke but they looked clean so why did they smell? I wonder how my mouth smells, like my finger that never really gets washed properly or the nail which is embedded with my leftovers, anyways I don't care.

I come downstairs dressed all in black for the first time in my life, as I always wear a colour with black and even though I can still smell last night's feast, there is silence, there is no splattering of eggs or the hiss of the kettle, the kitchen door is open and Father is not down and this has never happened before. What else will happen today that didn't before? I pick up a greenish-yellow banana. I like mine a bit raw rather than the ones that have brown dots on them, they might give me freckles on my face so I avoid those. I come back into the hall and Father's door is still closed so I shout "Bye father, I am going to uni, I'll be back in the evening." As I hitch the door to its loud latch, I put my hand in my coat pocket and smile, the coco butter hand cream and red lipstick are still safe with me.

I catch the tube and no, tubes don't travel during the night, and head off to uni. I get off the tube and slowly walk towards the campus with Mercy's picture now in my head. I am not looking at the footpath or the dozens of pedestrians and cars racing by. A woman with a black coat and grey umbrella passes by and I wonder when it's going to rain, but I have forgotten my umbrella, my hair will get wet and it will become frizzy and it will look a mess, but then my life is like that! I step onto my campus and I see a red umbrella held up high by a tall, slender woman, not a girl. I put my hand back into my pocket, the red lipstick is still there. I take it out and close my eyes and imagine the shape of my thick lips, white baboon lips and this time carefully apply the lipstick on them, not plaster it on.

"Mercy, Mercy, with the red umbrella, wait." No one turns back or listens expect for a young boy walking near me, small and good-looking, a bit like Anthony. I offer him something wise, "Get lost, why you looking at me?" but don't wait for a reply.

"Charming" is the only thing he

says. I see the still trees and yet there's wind in the air, streets are full yet I don't recognise anyone or any place and I don't know whether to be angry or ashamed so instead I take no notice and move on and then I breath in and out and knock on the big door whilst I get my breath back. For the first time ever, I stand at the side of the door so I cannot be seen but I have my ears to the keyhole and I can hear some fiddling to the door chain and a clearing of the throat and then slowly the door is fully open and Father is standing with an icy cold look on his face, it was much colder than the temperature outside. I quickly pushed him aside and brushed passed the rickety wall radiator which was warm and went straight into the kitchen as I sensed that something was happening in there, why else would he have been speechless?

I didn't look to see who was in

there, instead I went straight to the chair where she used to sit but someone had already taken the seat. I felt angry and I didn't even bother looking at the person sitting on that particular seat. My legs slowly started feeling like jelly and like my Father's good little child, I went and sat on my own seat, near my Father's seat. I could tell that he had been sitting there not that long ago because the fabric had ballooned with the weight and somehow it didn't look cold.

I kept looking at the door waiting for Father to come in but he didn't and yet I could sense within my body that he was standing on the other side of it and I continued to look at the crack to see a glimpse of him but saw nothing. My heart felt his existence behind the door almost as if I could smell his Brut aftershave mixed with the warmth of the central heating but today I could smell a female perfume and I wasn't wearing any. It was almost a powdery light smell, like a body spray, not perfume, not heavy. I could hear him sniffling now even though he had not entered into the kitchen and I hear a female crying, closer to me than he was. I kept looking at the door wishing Father would stop crying and enter, his left hand would be shaking now. I need to go to him and so I get up, take out the red lipstick from my pocket and the hand cream and go to the crying Mercy and put it in her lap, along with my tears and go to reach out to my father for the first time in a long time, maybe I don't need to remember the night train anymore.